SANDRA DAY O'CONNOR

CHICO

illustrated by **DAN ANDREASEN**

DUTTON CHILDREN'S BOOKS

DUTTON CHILDREN'S BOOKS
A division of Penguin Young Readers Group
Published by the Penguin Group
Penguin Group (USA) Inc., 375 Hudson Street, New York, New York 10014, U.S.A.
Penguin Group (Canada), 10 Alcorn Avenue, Toronto, Ontario, Canada M4V 3B2 (a division of Pearson Penguin Canada Inc.)
Penguin Books Ltd, 80 Strand, London WC2R 0RL, England
Penguin Ireland, 25 St Stephen's Green, Dublin 2, Ireland (a division of Penguin Books Ltd)
Penguin Group (Australia), 250 Camberwell Road, Camberwell, Victoria 3124, Australia (a division of Pearson Australia Group Pty Ltd)
Penguin Books India Pvt Ltd, 11 Community Centre, Panchsheel Park, New Delhi - 110 017, India
Penguin Group (NZ), Cnr Airborne and Rosedale Roads, Albany, Auckland 1310, New Zealand (a division of Pearson New Zealand Ltd)
Penguin Books (South Africa) (Pty) Ltd, 24 Sturdee Avenue, Rosebank, Johannesburg 2196, South Africa
Penguin Books Ltd, Registered Offices: 80 Strand, London WC2R 0RL, England

CIP Data is available.

Published in the United States by Dutton Children's Books,
a division of Penguin Young Readers Group
345 Hudson Street, New York, New York 10014
www.penguin.com/youngreaders

Designed by Gloria Cheng

Manufactured in China · First Edition
1 3 5 7 9 10 8 6 4 2
ISBN 0-525-47452-8

This book is dedicated to all children who love horses.

S.D.O.

Sandra lived on a ranch. The ranch was in the desert and was many miles away from any town.

There were no other children on the ranch, but Sandra wasn't lonely. She was six years old. She helped her father with the ranch chores, and she helped her mother in the kitchen. She often went to the barns and corrals with the cowboys to help feed the horses and the baby calves whose mothers could not be found. She knew where to find the eggs laid by the chickens and the kittens that lived in the barn. And she loved reading books in the long afternoons.

Sandra liked to explore the ranch and to look for rabbits, antelope, skunks, badgers, birds, and turtles. But she knew she should stay away from the sharp thorns on the cactus, and from scorpions and coyotes. And she was very careful to stay away from rattlesnakes.

Of all the animals on the ranch, Sandra liked horses best. She had learned how to sit on a horse before she could walk. Her father and some of the cowboys would take her up on the saddle with them to ride near the house. As soon as her legs were long enough to reach the stirrups, she could ride by herself.

When Sandra was five, her father gave her a small horse named Chico. Chico was very gentle and seemed to enjoy having a child ride on his back. Sandra learned how to put on his saddle and his bridle and how to get on Chico all by herself. She loved sitting high above the ground on her horse. He felt warm and strong. She learned how to make Chico go fast or slow. Once in a while, she tumbled off Chico and landed on the ground with a big BUMP! He would stop and wait for her to get back on again.

Sandra's parents said she could ride Chico in the pasture close to the house anytime she wanted. "Keep an eye out for rattlesnakes," her mother said. "Just watch where you are going and stay away from them. Then you won't get hurt."

Sandra rode Chico almost every day. Sometimes she pretended she was getting away from a horse thief, and she made Chico run fast. Sometimes she pretended she was a rodeo barrel racer, and she would race Chico around a tall cactus as fast as he could go. But most of the time she pretended she was a rancher, riding out to take care of the cattle.

One day Sandra heard her father say to the cowboys that one of their cows had a new baby calf.

"Where is she, Daddy?" Sandra asked.

"She is about two or three miles out in the east pasture, near the windmill," he said.

There were big windmills in each pasture to lift water up from the underground wells into troughs so the cattle could drink. The windmills turned their fans in the wind, just like Sandra's toy pinwheel. The fans turned the windmills' gears, and the rods moved up and down to pump the water. Clank . . . clank . . . clank . . . Sandra could always hear the windmills working in the distance.

Sandra went to the corral and put the saddle and bridle on Chico. Although the new calf was not in the pasture close to the house, she didn't think her parents would mind if she rode a little farther to see the calf. She climbed on Chico and rode out to the east pasture. Before long, she was a couple of miles from the house. She could no longer see the windmills or the barn. She had been to the east pasture many times with her father. She was sure she could find the windmill there. She talked to Chico, who put his ears up to listen. "Let's find the new baby calf, Chico."

Sandra always liked to see the little newborn calves. Their mothers would not let her come near, but she could wait quietly until the mother cow walked away to eat some grass or to get a drink of water. Then Sandra could pat the calf. The calves did not seem to be afraid.

Chico followed a path along a small canyon that led to the windmill. He wanted to get a drink of water from the trough, so he started to trot. There, not far away, was the cow with her new baby calf. The calf had curly red hair, a snow-white face, and a pink nose. It was so little that its legs wobbled when it stood up. The calf bawled for its mother. The mother cow licked her little calf and gave it some milk. Sandra wanted to pat the calf, but she knew the cow would not let her get close. So she sat quietly on Chico and watched until she thought it was time to go home for lunch.

Sandra turned Chico along a path on a hill where she had a view across the desert. Every creature she saw was looking for something to eat. The cows were looking for grass. The rabbits hopped along, looking for tender plants. Birds flew high in the sky, hoping to spot an insect or seeds on the ground. A coyote chased a rabbit. Sandra wished she had brought a sandwich to eat. Meanwhile, big clouds were forming in the sky—clouds that might get big enough to produce rain.

Sandra was not looking where Chico was walking. All of a sudden, Chico jumped. Then he stopped short and trembled with fear. Sandra almost fell off, but she held on to the saddle and the reins. "What's the matter, Chico?" she asked. Then she saw something that made her freeze in fright, too. On the ground ahead was a rattlesnake, coiled up and rattling its rattle, ready to strike and bite Chico's leg. Sandra knew Chico could die if he was bitten by a rattlesnake.

Sandra's heart beat very fast. She wanted to get away as quickly as she could. She gave Chico a big kick and pulled the reins hard to the right. Chico jumped to the side and began to run. Sandra couldn't wait to get home safely. "Hurry, Chico! Faster!" she yelled.

Chico ran like the wind, and soon they could see the ranch house, the windmills, and the barn. Sandra could see her parents near the barn. When they reached the corral, Sandra jumped down and took off Chico's saddle and bridle. His sides were wet with sweat, and he was breathing fast.

Sandra ran to her parents to tell them what had happened. Her father put his hand on her shoulder and said, "I am glad you and Chico are all right. Next time, be sure you always look where you and your horse are going, and watch out for things in your path."

"I will," she said. Then her father said, "Cool Chico down and give him some water. After lunch I have to go check on the water in the east pasture near where you rode this morning. We can see if the cow and calf are safe from the snake. Do you want to come along, Sandra?"

Sandra hesitated. She was scared of the snake, but she wanted to be a good rancher and protect the calf.

"Sure, Daddy. I'll go."

Sandra liked riding Chico, but it was always good to be with her father going somewhere on the ranch in the truck. They drove along the dusty, bumpy road to the east pasture.

"Do you see what I see?" asked her father.

"No. What? Where?" said Sandra.

"Over there by the hill. See the antelope? There are six of them."

Sure enough, Sandra could see six antelope in the distance. They were standing very still, all looking at the pickup truck, with their ears up tall and their tails up, too. Her father stopped the truck so they could watch. Suddenly, one of the antelope leaped high and began to run, and all the others followed. They ran with big, graceful leaps, like dancers in a ballet. Sandra was always excited to see antelope. She wished they would stand still and let her get closer, like the cows, but they never did.

Sandra's father parked the truck and began working on the water trough in the east pasture. Sandra walked to the place near the windmill where she had seen the little calf that morning. It was lying there. The mother cow was some distance away, eating grass. This time Sandra was able to pat the calf and rub its forehead. She did not see the rattlesnake anywhere around the calf, and she was happy that the little calf was safe. Then her father called for her to come back to the truck. It was late afternoon, and they started home.

Meanwhile the clouds had grown larger and darker. Now there was no blue sky left at all. The wind began to blow, carrying dust and leaves up into the air. A bolt of lightning struck the ground not far from their truck. The sound of thunder rolled through the clouds. Sandra snuggled closer to her father. The lightning and thunder frightened her. The first few drops of rain splashed on the windshield, making muddy streaks. Then the rain fell harder and faster. Soon the rain was falling so hard they had to stop the truck and just watch and listen.

"Oh dear, Daddy, there is water and mud everywhere," said Sandra. "Do you think the baby calf will be all right?"

"Don't mind that," he said. "Rain is what we need and want most. Don't ever complain about that. Rain makes the grass grow. The cows need grass to eat. Everything at the ranch needs the rain—even the new baby calf."

Finally the rain slowed to a sprinkle, and Sandra could see out the truck windows again. Everything had changed. Muddy water was running down every little hill and into every ditch. The bushes and grass all sparkled with drops of water, and the air smelled fresh and good.

Rabbits were peeking out of their burrows, and the birds began to chirp. In the sky a big rainbow formed with colors of red, blue, green, and yellow.

"Daddy, let's go find the pot of gold at the end of the rainbow," said Sandra. "It's right over there!"

"All right," said her father. "Maybe we'll find it, just like you found the baby calf this morning. But we can only go for a little while, because your mother will be worried about us if we are gone too long."

As they drove toward the rainbow, it seemed to move farther away. Sandra's father said, "We have to get home now. It is almost dark."

When they got back to the house, Sandra ran inside to tell her mother about all they had seen. Then she went to check on Chico. She got a big handful of hay to give to him. While he chewed, Sandra patted his neck and said, "Thank you, Chico, for getting me home safely today. We were lucky, weren't we? Good night now. I'll see you tomorrow."

When Sandra got into her bed that night, she listened to the frogs that lived in the mud of the pond. They always croaked at night after a hard rain. She could hear the cow mooing to her calf and the clank of the windmills.

Her parents came in to say good night. "You are learning to be a good little ranch hand, Sandra," said her father. "Don't you run into any rattlesnakes in your dreams."

"All right, Daddy," Sandra said. And she fell asleep dreaming about riding Chico to find the pot of gold at the end of the rainbow.